RAINE OF DARK FORTUNE

SUSAN STRADIOTTO

BRONZEWOOD books

Eden Prairie, MN

Raine of Dark Fortune

Published by
Bronzewood Books
14920 Ironwood Ct.
Eden Prairie, MN 55346

Cover Design: MIBLART & Bronzewood Books

eBook ISBN: 978-1-949357-52-3

Paperback ISBN: 978-1-949357-53-0

Interior Design: Bronzewood Books

Edited by: Melissa Kulis

RAINE

A GREAT AND TERRIBLE FORTUNE

RAINE ABARTA, FESTIVAL DIVINER AT the Wickney-area Renaissance Festival, held out his hands and bowed deeply before a trio of revelers. Hopefully, these three would be his next clients. "Miladies, My Lord." He held out a hand to the drunker of the two women, the one dressed as a belly dancer with a heaving bosom. Her hips jingled and soft curves defined her midsection. Glassy-eyed, she appraised Raine's glamoured form and swayed over to put her hand in his. Clearly, she believed *she*, rather than Raine, was the one putting on the show.

He had just awoken from a nap, sober to his dismay. A condition he needed to remedy quickly. Raine's mouth watered for a fix, and these three were primed for the taking. So, let the performance begin!

"May I gaze into your future, milady?" he asked, pitching his voice into a lilt most humans incorrectly understood to be a Renaissance-era European accent. He flourished a hand toward his sign, a gaudy thing above the door to his wagon reading Realm Diviner, Fortunes from the Fae. "'Tis a modest price to see what lies ahead." He placed a kiss on the belly-dancer's knuckles to top the performance.

The second woman giggled, lifted her cream-colored skirts, and bounced over to her friend's side. "Oohhh, Margo! You found the fortune teller. We did this last summer, remember?"

Apparently, it hadn't been remarkable, because Raine had no memory of these women or the man accompanying them. He bowed to her then. "I'm ashamed to say, Milady, but I can't recall. Perhaps my memory wanes after so many visions from the goddess Danu herself. Do you recall the result?"

This woman was blonde and taller than the first, and her red and gold corset gave the appearance of an hourglass figure. Although, Raine suspected she was as shapely as a stone column underneath. Yet she seemed far more animated than the first. She placed a hand on his arm. "You predicted my divorce." A dark, smoky gray misted through her aura—sadness fading away.

Raine recoiled, a hand over his chest and gasping—the proper response when a human announces their divorce. He paused in the pose, then leaned back toward her. "I do hope that wasn't a misfortune for you."

"Not at all." She waved her arm in a wide arc, her eyes widening and rolling with her words. "Best two-hundred pounds I ever lost."

"Oh. So relieved to hear," he said. "I hate to be the bearer of tragic news. I do hope you'll honor me with the opportunity to divine your fortune again."

Sudden giddiness flashed brightly through her aura, like a woman walking into Bath and Body Works, and she clapped her hands. "Yes, yes! Of course. All three of us."

Raine inhaled her outpour of emotion. The best thing about working at the Ren Fest: he got a steady fix of human levity—the strongest drug imaginable for a faerie—while making enough money to carry him through the winter months until he could get back to his street-performing gig in Wickney Square. Margo and the other woman nearly fizzed with mirth, but Raine focused on the divorcee. Margo's breath reeked of mead, so siphoning her levity could be dangerous if Raine took too much. A nice high was good. A sloppy drunk one? Well by Danu, he'd probably lose his glamour and scare the poor human festival patrons with his freakish appearance.

Well, perhaps not . . . because if there were freaks to be found in Wickney, the Ren Fest had them.

A man stepped closer behind the two women, somber. He held a tankard from the leather-worker's shop and wore the simplest of costumes: brown breeches and a tan, unadorned tunic. However, he apparently couldn't be bothered with appropriate footwear given the bright red swoosh on his Nikes.

"Ah, sir." Raine attempted to humor the man. "These lasses must be in your charge?"

The man grunted, and the blonde woman pushed at his arm and pleaded, "Come on, Devlin. You're far too serious. It'll be fun."

Still silent, Devlin gave a reluctant nod. Margo went to the man's side while the other woman trotted toward the steps into Raine's wagon.

Raine jumped to intercept her. "Wait, wait. Allow me to get that for you, Milady." He pulled a hand broom from beneath the wagon and waggled it before her.

Properly chastened, the woman in the corset straightened her spine as Raine swept off the already clean steps. He unlatched the red door and placed one hand on the small of his back, offering the other to her. Prim- and proper-like, she pushed her chin high and laid her hand lightly in Raine's waiting palm. He tipped his head forward and assisted her into the wagon.

The belly dancer's foot fumbled on the steps, but Devlin caught her before she toppled onto the ground. Once he'd seen her safely inside, the man stared expectantly at Raine. He either felt far less intoxicated than the other two or held his alcohol more somberly, the brooding-but-silent type. Whichever the case, his stony façade didn't suit Raine's needs. Devlin presented a challenge, and Raine felt certain that once Devlin found a smidgen of humor, he'd emit the sweetest drug to feed Raine's Faerie addiction. That was always the case. When a human's mood turned from foul to fair, well, just yum. Raine shuddered to think of how sweet it would be.

With a grin, Raine *nudged* him a little—another one of his many Fae gifts. "Kind sir, would you join us for a bit of conversation and perhaps refreshment?"

Succumbing to the faerie wiles, the man's brow relaxed. He nodded once and climbed the rickety wooden steps.

Raine took a final gander around the grounds and the crowd. Twilight quickly approached night, but the drum jam signaling the day's close wouldn't come for another hour, maybe more.

Stepping inside, Raine drew the door on the back of his wagon closed, then took his seat behind a tiny desk with a glass orb bubbling up beneath a purple velvet blanket. "Margo, Devlin, welcome to my divination chamber." Raine side-eyed the blonde suggestively. "Again, I must apologize for not remembering you, Milady. May I ask your name? I find it easier to divine fortunes once I know your given name."

Margo swayed a little in her seat, distracting both women. They giggled among themselves, and when he had their attention again, Raine blew Margo a kiss. Before he could turn back to the woman in ivory, the man's aura flared—struck through with red-hot anger.

Ah, quite the reaction, thought Raine. *So, Margo is the one he claims.* "No insult intended, My Lord," Raine hurried to say. "Please, do have a seat next to your lovely mistress." He motioned to the third and only remaining empty stool.

While Devlin took his seat, the corseted woman's giggling ebbed. "Aahhh," she sighed, holding herself around the waist. "I'm Jana."

Raine tipped his head in a nod toward her. "Thanks," the gesture said, and he spread his hands, palms up, to either side. *Let the show begin.* He tipped his face upward, as so many do when speaking to the gods. He couldn't be sure why; in truth, it seemed quite cliché to him. But it's what everyone expected, so he played the part.

He paused and let the tension build. "Beautiful Faerie Goddess, Danu, join us here, in this inner holy sanctum." He made his voice grand, bellowing. "Show me the fates of Devlin, of Margo, and of Jana." Then he paused for dramatic effect and suddenly dropped his arms to the side and bowed his head as if struck into a trance.

A subtle rustling of the three humans turning to look at one another reached his ears, and one woman whisper-slurred, "Whash 'appening?"

"Shh. This is normal," Jana, he felt certain, hissed back.

Raine pushed a hand forward to silence them, keeping

his head bowed. "Be patient. It can take a moment for the Goddess to share her will." This, he said, stalling and giving himself enough time to shift his glamour.

When he raised his head, his clients would see a new vision of him—his eyes pearly white with no irises or pupils. Most believed it was a sleight of hand that he slipped in contacts while his head was lowered. Wouldn't they be terrified if they knew it was real Fae magic?

In a jerk, he lifted his head and opened his eyes. Their gasps of delight and fear stirred his craving. "Danu chooses you." He pointed to Devlin, selecting the most reluctant of the party. The choice always made for a better show. "Your hand please, My Lord."

Devlin furrowed his brow.

Jana bounced up from the stool and stood behind him, hands caressing his shoulders. "Go on, Dev. Just a little fun."

Margo looped her hand under his elbow, urging his arm forward. "Play along, babe."

Ah, thought Raine, *we have a thruple.* "Yes *Dev, babe,*"—he pitched his voice higher, cooing—"the White Lady Danu, Goddess of all of Faerie, asks for you to give me your hand so that she may see and allow me to divine your fortune."

With a look over his shoulder at Jana, then at Margo, he visibly decided to humor his women and held out his non-drink hand to Raine.

"The Goddess thanks you," Raine said, bowing his head so that his headscarf almost touched their joined hands. Devlin had given him his left hand, the wedding band prominent, and Raine fleetingly wondered which one was the wife, if either. Perhaps he'd find that out in the visions, so Raine focused his senses on the task.

Walking through memories took something from the Fae who attempted it, changed them for a while and gave them characteristics of the person they delved into. The one time he'd done it with someone too aged, he hadn't been sure his hip would ever feel the same. However, given his faerie constitution, he'd recovered after a few days. Fortunately, Devlin appeared hale enough, strong even. And not too drunk. Raine couldn't do such a thing with Margo, because he'd be slurring the rest of the divination and he might not be able to get in any more clients for the day. But stepping into the man's shoes might give Raine a little boost in energy—especially if Devlin planned on servicing two women after the Ren Fest. If Margo wasn't so intoxicated, he might be jealous of the human. But then again, Fae and humankind were a dangerous combo in bed.

In the darkness behind Raine's closed eyes, images emerged. The Faerie Goddess had no hand in this; memory walking was simply a talent all faeries could access when needed. The unfortunate part was that he witnessed each scene through the eyes of the person he touched. Now, as the image formed, he saw another man, someone who could be a younger version of Devlin himself. But then Devlin's blood-covered hands reached out and grabbed the man by the shirt. No ring. So this had been some time before now. Devlin jerked the guy's shirt, pulling him close. "Drayke, what the fuck is wrong with you?"

This had to be Devlin's brother. Heat flared in Raine's chest, a reflection of Devlin's rage focused on Drayke. The edges of the vision turned red, and there were legs, feminine and naked, lying on the cobblestone behind the front-and-center face. Raine tried to turn the focus to see more of the background, but to no avail.

Devlin turned the man, throwing him into the backseat of a car, shouting, "I told you never again!" then slamming the door. In the reflection, Raine could see Devlin's face simmering with fury, but with fewer lines at the corners of his eyes. A streak of blood painted a path on one side of his forehead. The reflection heaved as Devlin breathed deeply, trying to calm himself.

Shite! Raine dropped Devlin's hand, cutting the vision short. It didn't appear that Devlin would be turning around quickly, and Raine wanted out of that mess. Faced with this new conundrum, he was convinced he'd invited the wrong people inside. This vision would throw him right back into his little tango with the Wickney Police Department. Yeah, he missed giving the skinny rookie Vic a hard time and "working out" with Harley on occasion, but he had promised Vic and Harley's ranking officer Ken he would stay away for a while. Kennedi Craine had begged him to give her the time to find some kind of normalcy in her new life after their last case together. But that vision. He wouldn't be able to let it go entirely, because it tickled his Fae*dìom*, or so he called it. The real name for the Fae obsession with puzzles of all kinds was *dìomhaireachdanseòlta,* but that was a mouthful. The problem would probably tickle Ken's Fae*dìom* too, even though she was only half–Fae.

Regardless, he needed to pull himself out of these thoughts. He had a performance to maintain at the moment and the rest of today's festival to close out. And seeing a crime sometime in the past wouldn't help him give any fun news to the thruple in his wagon presently. But Raine also needed to catch his breath, because this guy he'd just memory walked with had to be the horniest human alive. Everything he was physically seemed keyed around sex, and that had Raine uncomfortably hard.

"Well?" Jana prompted, but Raine didn't look up.

The man grunted, then barked, "Hey!" When Raine still didn't answer, he continued, "Uh, Mister Fortuneteller? You gonna predict my future?"

Now the jerk sounded downright snarky, and Raine couldn't have any of that. He'd taken note of the wedding ring on Devlin's finger and noted the absence of one on Jana's. And he'd noticed how Jana seemed a little more close to Devlin than Margo. So he ventured a guess that this thruple wasn't all fun and games. Time to nip the human's attitude right in the bud.

Raine let his irises swirl a little and looked up at Devlin.

Rightly so, the man recoiled slightly.

"You and your *wife* recently had a fight, am I right?" Raine quirked his brow.

The man and drunk woman exchanged a look.

"I'll take that as a yes," said Raine, flourishing a hand and looking up at Jana.

For some reason, probably that she wanted this pathetic human man all to herself, her aura flared. Raine siphoned off a little of her excitement and thrill over the mention of the fight and smirked at Devlin.

"Well." Raine inhaled deeply to calm his body and resumed his act. "The only news Danu gives me today is that there's a rather indulgent make-up experience and more awaiting you this evening. I must say, Devlin, you're quite the lucky man with two women to satisfy your needs. The vision got me a little hot and bothered, so I'll ask for my fee and spend a few moments . . . ahem . . . alone." Raine flexed his left hand meaningfully in front of his face and winked at Devlin.

That news, apparently, was good enough to have the

man pulling out his wallet.

Money in hand, Raine opened the door and followed the man outside. He helped Jana down first, then offered a hand to Margo. Unbidden, a vision flashed in Raine's mind. A picture of Devlin and the other man, Drayke, hovering over her, both splattered with blood.

Raine felt cold and thirsty. He'd felt that sensation before—the reason a faerie never memory walked with the dead. This was the first sign of life leaving a human's body.

He dropped her hand like a hot iron kettle, leaned in, and whispered, "You might not want to be alone with . . ." He flicked his eyes at Devlin. "Especially if there's another man with him."

"Isssat jealousy talkin'?" Margo draped herself around Raine. "Yyyou wanna join usss after the drums? Foursome?"

Raine peeled her arms from around his neck, fighting the urge to curl his lip in revulsion, and scanned the crowd for his next vict—er, clients. "I have more work," he lied. He didn't have his next clients yet, but he hoped to make another hundred or so before closing. Furthermore, the puzzle he'd seen in these two visions no longer sounded like much fun. "You run along. But heed your fortune."

Raine spun away, stripping the scarf from his head and running a hand through his bronze chin-length hair. He needed to walk off that interaction, perhaps mingle a little with some of the other revelers. But he stopped sharply after only three steps when he spotted two women dressed in the authentic fashion of the old-world, the time before the gods turned against one another and split the realms. When these women emerged from the gathered humans, darkness shimmered in midnight blue around them. It seemed more like a swirling mist from the Darkness itself than the light in human auras.

Raine's kind, the Fae, while they might enjoy a little manipulation in the name of good fun, were of the Light. Warm and bronzed from Danu's realm where light fell like snowflakes from the skies.

Those two made his heart plummet into his gut. They were of the Dark.

Aodh's faithful.

Myla

The Eve of Bonding

GLOAMING HAD SETTLED OVER THE festival grounds, daylight giving way to darkness. Finally.

"*Dùin*," Myla said to close off the stream of magic feeding her daylight-shielding spell. Because she was a witch of the Darkness, the light otherwise blinded her and singed her skin. The Renaissance Festival had been fun so far, reminiscent of the markets from the time before she'd become one of the Dracagard, protectors of the dragons of old. However, concentration on maintaining the spell had also limited her ability to relax on the evening before she promised herself to Emrys for the rest of her life, a millennium or more. Since she no longer had to concentrate on the spell, the mead she had consumed throughout the day began to lighten Myla's spirits and loosen her inhibitions. More than once while watching the belly dancers or dancing herself to the Uilleann Pipe- and Fiddle-ensembles, Myla believed she saw piskies playing pranks, rollicking, and celebrating amid the modern-day unsuspecting humans. One man might have lost his keys today, a woman . . . a hat, all to the delight of the tiniest of the greenwood creatures.

That can't be, she admonished herself. *Only a figment of your imagination.* That was the old magic, and she had never heard of the tiny folk following them to the new lands. Although . . . tomorrow marked the autumnal equinox, a time when the barriers between the living world and the dead began thinning as Samhain approached. Once upon a time, the smallest sidhe would still have been at play.

Several paces away from her sister Malin, Myla shook her head, blinking to clarify the image, and yes—the small yellow lights blinking in the distance were no more than fireflies. She sighed, wishing for the days when the creatures weren't forced into hiding as a result of fear and superstition. Myla took another swig of the strawberry mead and froze when a somewhat modest cart with a red door caught her eye.

She wiped away a dribble from her chin and bounced the few steps to Malin's side. Myla tugged playfully at her sister's bell-shaped sleeve. "Look, Malin!" She pointed to the small wooden wagon. The sign above the round door on the rear read, Festival Diviner, Fortunes from the Fae. "If the proprietor has any connection to the Fae, she may be able to read the threads of time and give an accurate view into the future. I have faith in my match, Emrys, but it would settle the nerves to know what to expect on the morrow." Intoxication had her slipping back into the more traditional ways of speaking, but fortunately, here, everyone was pretending to be from another time.

Malin scowled at her, always the more serious twin. "Myla, you know what to expect. The bonding rites are well recorded in our histories, and we've witnessed more than a dozen ourselves."

Why did she have to be so practical? Myla slouched at the shoulders, pouting. "Where's your sense of adventure?

What do the humans here know of Fae or faeries? If she has even a drop of Fae blood, it's nothing but luck that she's discovered her divination skills."

Her sister stopped, pulling Myla by their interlaced arms to turn and face her. "Since when do you invite faerie tricks or the goddess of the Light realm into your life?" Malin's violet eyes, an almost identical replica of her own, burned a hole through her.

Myla allowed her head to fall backward momentarily and huffed. There she went with another warning about the lines between realms. With a gesture toward the fortuneteller's den, she turned back to Malin. "Whoever is in that wagon probably isn't a real faerie." In Wickney, where there were gates between the Daylight realm and both the realms of Light and Dark, many creatures walked amid the mortals. But relations between them were forbidden by all the gods—excepting the case where a human was born with the nimh, the extra gland that marked them as one of Aodh's children. Myla doubted the diviner was Fae. She may have known one of Danu's children, but the chances of a Faerie deigning to work here—or anywhere—were nil.

"Wicca and Fae don't mix, Myla—even half-bloods or impostors."

"You are far too stoic." Myla put out her bottom lip. "We are supposed to be celebrating. Isn't this what the mortals call a bachelorette party? We left our dragons behind so we could be a little careless tonight, right?" Myla spread her hands, palms up, and spun in a slow circle under the early evening moonlight. "We only have an hour of the festival left, so let's make the most of it." She folded her hands beneath her chin, pleading with her sister.

Malin jutted her hip. "I'm happy to dance at the drum

jam, but tempting Aodh's ire for consorting with her enemy, no way. And the fact that I don't have Breyze and you don't have Aemro also means we're not equipped to head into a battle. We need to blend in, *be* mortal tonight."

"Fine. I'll go without you." She threw up her arms and whirled around, calling quietly over her shoulder, "It's what a mortal would do."

Malin caught her by the wrist. "Oh, no you don't." She set her mouth in a tight line and dropped her brow. "You win, but only because you're about to go through bonding. This stays quiet. Emrys, having been selected to become one of the Dark Mother's acolytes, will have my heart on a stick if he finds out I let you gallivant with Fae tricksters."

Myla skipped toward her sister, holding her half–full mug of mead away so she could lean forward ballet–style on one foot. She pecked her sister on the cheek. "Knew you'd let me have my fun. Besides, Fae are only different, not the enemy. That dishonor is reserved for semaphor slime, remember? Let's go!" They started toward the wagon, together, Malin grumbling at Myla's side. But despite her rumbles or their disagreement, both knew the false light–bearers, those who called themselves semaphors, were the truest enemy to all gods and goddesses regardless of alliance. Light, Dark, Sea, Shore, Forest, Hunt. If they had a shared foe, it was the semaphors.

At the wagon door, Myla first searched for the chimes, the traditional method of requesting divination services. Finding none, she smirked at Malin and knocked on the doors. Truly, the proprietor had to be naught but an actress, because this showed no signs of a true seer.

"Madam Diviner?" she called.

Silence.

"Good. The Dark Mother watches out for her children." Malin turned her mug upside down, two drops drizzling out. "Let's find another mead before the stands close."

"Not so fast."

Malin dropped her arms, clearly resigning herself.

"Here." Myla shoved her half-full mug into her sister's hands. "Drink mine. I'm going in."

"You haven't been invited . . . Myla!"

But it was too late. She'd already entered. The interior was small, though larger than should be possible if the Diviner had no magic. *Perhaps*, Myla thought. *No, impossible.* It wasn't anything more than an optical illusion. A seer would not have the implements of the impostors: Tarot cards, a cauldron, a poster humans believed was a third eye, colorful rocks passed off as magic crystals, or the laughable glass ball on the table at center focus. No. Whoever this was was acting. Myla lifted the velvet cloth that covered the so-called crystal ball. "Mal, c'mon. It's just a show."

As her sister stepped inside, Myla ran her fingers over the glass. Malin looked around, her shoulders visibly dropping, easing with each little sight she took in.

Myla plopped down in the chair behind the table. "We'll wait. She'll surely be back shortly."

Gulping the mead, Malin eased onto one of the stools across the table. No sooner than her backside hit the cushion than the wagon's doors slammed shut with not so much as a bounce. She glared at Myla.

"Just the wind. Try it."

Malin reached behind her and pushed on the doors.

Nothing. They wouldn't budge.

RAINE

THE GODDESS SPEAKS

THOSE TWO HEADED MY WAY . . . that's a whole crap-ton of nope-nope, no way in Danu's Sanctuary or Aodh's Dark Dungeon! Faeries and dark witches don't mix. Raine had once believed that was merely a false tale from the old country. Gods and goddesses could be petty that way, hoarding their children close to their chest. But after his "dear" mother sent him to spend some time in the Dark, he'd learned his lesson.

Nope-nope!

Raine hid behind his cart and watched. Twins. Why did they have to be twins? Because of that, their magic would be stronger than most of their kind. However, they were out before full darkness had settled over Wickney, so they couldn't have brought their familiars. And with his *sight*, the faerie gift that allowed him to see and read emotions and magic, he could tell they were weaker tonight than usual. Only a hint of the characteristic blue smoky aura wisping around them. They also didn't wear the characteristic attire of the Dracagard—no cloaks of darkness, tight leathers, or boots for ass-kicking. No, they wore dresses in the Old Irish fashion, perhaps even ones preserved from the time of his youth. That vision warmed him inside. Maybe he could return to Fae and visit that little village that held on to the ways of old.

What in Danu's name are you thinking, Raine?

Queen Amaryllis, also known as Mommy-dearest, wouldn't allow him any peace in Faerie. He shivered from head to toe at the thought and refocused on the witches.

One seemed cheery, bubbly, some might say. She was clearly trying to pull the scowling one toward his cart. Raine rooted for the other one. *C'mon Crabby Pants, convince your sister it's a bad idea.* Hopefully, she'd take her twin and go somewhere, anywhere else. His day had been going so good before his nap. Now he had another murder puzzle to obsess over and a couple of dark witches eying up his Ren Fest "stage." He narrowed his eyes, trying to *nudge* the bubbly sister into not wanting to come inside.

Clearly, it wouldn't work from this distance, because she kissed her sister on the cheek and pulled her toward his wagon.

Alone behind the back wooden wheel, he lifted his face to the darkening sky, hands held wide. "Why Danu?"

Silence fell, the crowd noises vanishing.

Chimes rang in the air—*tling, tling,* the sound characteristic of Sanctuary in Fae. "Because you are my connection," an ethereal voice, delicately laced and dancing on the soft breeze, answered.

The area behind his cart began to glow, also like

the holy grounds in Fae. Ever-so-slowly, he settled his eyes onto the Faerie Goddess Danu standing before him, knots forming in his gut.

Tling, tling. "Do not worry, my child, no one will see us." Danu spread her arms from the point where she stood before him. Well, floated in a kind of ghostly manner would be a much more accurate description.

"Creepy," he said. "Can you tone it down a mite?"

A smile spread across her features, but Raine felt a warning in his *croí*. The goddess was the image of celestial perfection—button nose, big eyes, perpetually puckered lips, hair of gold animated by a wind that only touched her. Despite the warning, she dimmed her light and settled into a form that appeared normal for this realm. Almost. The way her eyes and hair still radiated was anything but human.

The sound of Raine's wagon doors closing made him jump.

Danu waited until he set his eyes back upon her. "My doing," she answered his unspoken question. "They entered, but I sealed the doors. They may now only be opened by one of the Fae."

"Wha—Who?" Raine pressed his lips together. There were no others of the Fae here, so for him. The doors to free the witches could now only be opened by him.

Beating resounded from inside.

"We need them to remain within until I can use you to deliver our message."

Raine plunged his hands into his hair, paused, then narrowed his eyes. "Wait. Who is *we*?"

"Unimportant." Danu flicked a hand dismissively. "What is important is that you go into your . . . abode?"

"My cart of fortunes, naturally."

Tling, tling. A smile graced Danu's face again. "Well, child, you will need to enter and converse with the children of Aodh. Deliver their fortunes, if you will." *Tling, tling.*

Danu was gone, and the sounds of the Ren Fest resumed.

"Shite!" He stomped a foot and pouted for a second like he'd seen more than one spoiled child do. First, he'd been roped into some human drama—twice. Then Danu appeared to him, something no one had heard of since the last Fae Kings ruled the courts of the seasons before his lovely mother had overthrown them. And now he was teaming up with the Dark? Groaning, he decided: if he had to help the witches, maybe he could get an IOU in the form of a spell. Man, he was brilliant.

A knocking sounded again from within the wagon.

"Keep your skirts on." Raine circled to the entrance, took a deep breath, and barged inside, closing the doors behind him.

It knocked the crabby sister backward. "Fuck! Myla, it *is* a faerie." She shielded her eyes as she assumed a fighting stance, or as much as she could in the cramped quarters.

"Ha!" Raine barked, folding his arms across his chest. "You look ridiculous." He let the Fae magic course through his veins and intensified his glamour to dull the natural radiance of his race.

Crabby appeared confused. Although she clearly took his action as a sign he meant them no harm because she eased her stance. "Uh, we'll just let you be," she tried.

Raine blocked her path. "Not so fast. I'm only here

because the goddess sent me."

Her brows drew together at that. "That makes no—"

Myla shoved her body into her sister's side, her eyes wide. "You mean *Danu* sent you to *us*?"

He folded his arms over his chest. "Now you're getting it. You must be the smart one."

Crabby side-eyed him. "No. It doesn't make sense. You know who, and what, we are?"

"Well,"—he shrugged—"She's Myla, and although I've named you *Crabby*, I'm sure you have another name."

Her jaw dropped, but words didn't immediately spew forth. Speechless perfection.

Raine smirked. Their names weren't what she meant, and he knew it. Didn't hurt to toy with her though. Everyone knew faeries had to have their fun or they'd die a slow and grueling death.

"She's Malin," Myla offered, a bit too eagerly and cutting off her sister's hanging objection.

Malin closed her mouth, clearly willing herself to have patience with her sister, but she raised her brows in an expectant glare. "And you are?"

"I am"—he stuck out a hand and cocked a grin—"right as . . . *Raine*."

Both sisters groaned, but Malin spoke up first. "So, tell us why Danu sent you, and we'll be on our way."

"Have a seat." He motioned to the empty stools and circled around to take his far more comfortable chair. He yanked the purple velvet from the glass ball sitting on a pedestal on the tiny desk. "I can't tell your fortunes if I don't look into my trusty crystal ball."

Myla sat, smiling, and patted the empty stool next to her. Reluctantly, her sister sank onto the cushion too.

"Alrighty then." Raine circled his hands above the ball and closed his eyes, not knowing what in the Darkness he was doing. "Danu, if you're still here, show me the futures for Aodh's daughters, these twins of the Dracagard."

Suddenly, light crashed into Raine. He felt warm and floating in whiteness. The only sounds to reach his ears were the *tling, tling,* and drizzling waters—the sounds of Sanctuary.

Malin

Beware of Vengeance

THIS WAS ALL WRONG. ONE of the Fae should never approach a Dark Witch. Now, as she watched the faerie hover his hands above the globe and put on quite the show of invoking his goddess, she tasted metal and her jaws hurt from clenching her teeth. Malin sat on the edge of the stool, forward from her sister and ready to leap up and protect them both physically if it came to that. She no longer felt Breyze's magic running through her veins and regretted not bringing her dragon. Myla could have gone without Aemro, but they were foolish to have crossed the borders between realms without some kind of magic protection. This show was proving her instincts right at every turn.

Suddenly, Raine's eyes flew open. Malin squinted. He'd toned down his natural faerie fire, but his eyes and hair now glowed with what looked like gold glitter under a spotlight. It burned the backs of Malin's eyes.

Tling, tling, a sound jingled.

"I apologize, daughters of Darkness. But being made of Light, this is as dim as I can be."

Myla squealed but cast her eyes downward toward the glass ball. Was the mead still dulling her senses? Malin laced her fingers with her sisters, ready to dart out of the wagon at any sign of danger.

"I mean you no harm," the goddess in Raine's body said. "I assure you of that."

"Why have you sought us out?" Malin kept her gaze away from Danu's. "Why not speak with the Dark Mother herself?"

Tling, tling. "I cannot enter the Dark realm, and my sister goddess Aodh has not surfaced from the Penumbra in a millennium. And without your familiars, you've provided me an ideal opportunity. I will be brief and share any other information with the faerie I now possess. He works with the police department in Wickney on occasion, and you may often find him performing in Wickney Square."

During the night? Malin wondered.

"Ah, yes. Please forgive me; I forget. He also frequents a club by the name of the Local, I believe, during the dark hours."

Malin rolled her eyes. *Yeah, Faerie-effin-central.* And it made her skin crawl that the goddess could hear both spoken and unspoken thought.

Danu continued, "There will be a shift between Light and Dark. It is now at the edge of my sight. You, Malin, are at its center." She paused for a long moment. *Tling, tling,* chimes rang again. Then she changed her course. "Princess Myla, I wish you a happy bonding in Darkness and newlywed year."

"Thank you, Lady Danu." Myla sounded as if she were at Dark Haven, praying to their goddess of Darkness instead of the patron of the Fae.

Malin's brow felt heavy. Not at the news of a shift or her being pivotal to the situation, for given her mother's advanced age, she and Myla would inherit the coven before many more years. But she didn't want to consider High Priestess Minerva's passing into Nèamh yet.

Regardless, Danu's well-wish seemed to have another message buried within. "Is there a reason you do not speak plainly, Goddess Danu?"

"Share this news with Aodh, for I fear we may need to work together in the end." *Tling, tling.* "That is all, Malin and Myla, Twins of Darkness."

Raine's head drooped.

The glow around him ceased. He leveled his gaze on Malin, blinking, with eyes wide and unfocused as if he just gained oodles of new knowledge in an instant. He jerked and shivered and shook his head. His eyes moved deliberately from Myla to Malin and back.

The doors to the cart swung open with a long creak, and the drums started outside. Raine clapped his hands and started rummaging around in the bins behind his desk. "So then, you have the message. Now we should all go dance. Where is my Tabor?" He tossed random items out as he looked.

"Ah . . ." Malin started.

"Go!" the faerie snapped.

Malin pulled Myla, who seemed calmer now and almost dazed, from her seated position and pushed her out before taking one last glance back at Raine.

Raine stood straight. "Wait! A word, Malin?" When she paused before descending the steps, he rushed over and clutched her forearms. A heavy burden seemed to weigh him down. "Beware of vengeance. I can't tell you more than this: Hard times will follow, but know that there will be someone strong in your future. One who will fight for Darkness. He's a match for your soul and you'll be a balm for one another's rage."

Malin pulled away, suddenly wary.

Raine returned to his bins, and she watched for a second in thorough confusion over how he shifted so quickly. Less than a minute later, he produced the drum and struck it three times, waggling his brows. "Let's go have a little fun at the drum jam!"

MYLA

AWAKENING

THE BEDDING COCOONED MYLA IN warmth, soft sheets rubbing like velvet against her naked body as she made the first tiny movements of the evening. She lay on her side, resting one arm on top of the weighted blanket. She kept her eyes closed, because it had to be too early for her to rise and greet the night. Between the strawberry honey-wine at the festival yesterday and all the dancing she'd done at both the drum jam and Club Infinity afterward, she felt the edge of soreness in every muscle in her body. Quite similar, in truth, to waking after her coven had spent a full night training to fight as a team.

In the bed next to her, Emrys must have sensed her rising from the depths of a long day's sleep, because the covers moved slightly as his weight shifted the bed. A second later, Myla felt his lips warming the inside of her wrist.

Kiss. "Good evening, my dark bride."

She could hear the smile and desire in his voice. Feel it as he kissed her arm, moving upward. Myla stretched and purred.

His breath felt hot against her skin. "There are no words in the old tongue or the new to describe how gorgeous you look just before you wake." Kiss. Kiss. He fluttered his lips against her shoulder, then her neck. "Aodh has blessed me by bringing me into the Dark as your *pháirtí*."

Eyes still closed, Myla wrapped her arm around her mate's shoulder and laced her fingers into the long hair at the back of his neck—she loved it when he woke with it free from its normal binding. "You flatter me." She sighed. "How the All Mother has really blessed you is by accepting you as one of her Darklings, my love. Your medical knowledge and work at Dark Haven—" Myla's eyes flew open. Recalling the message from the goddess of light, she pushed at Emrys's shoulders. "I need to find Mal and get to Dark Haven. I have a message—"

Emrys hushed her and swept a strand of hair off her forehead. "It's early yet. Your sister's likely still asleep." He dipped his head and kissed her collarbone again. "We have time for us first."

She hesitated, but then . . . "Mmm." Myla rolled her eyes back into her head, wanting nothing more than him. Tonight, the night of their Bonding in Darkness, was supposed to be about them, and them alone. She'd already started feeling all liquid-like and warm inside, so if they had a while . . . "*How* early?"

"At least an hour before first meal. Maybe two." He ran a tongue up her neck to her chin and then claimed her mouth. All worries of Danu's message vanished as his velvety tongue stroked hers, demanding her attention.

How could she resist as the smell of her mate enveloped her? Crisp and smoky like a cool autumn evening in the woods near a fire, it reminded her of the time when druids danced around open flame on the sabbats. She returned his demands, gently at first, then deepening, and their kisses drove her mad with desire. Even after all the years they'd been together, she still felt a pull stronger than gravity toward her pháirtí, the one person who so completely filled her heart. And not for the first time, she wondered how she'd gone so many decades without him at her side, but Aodh's dark witches age much slower than humans. Once Emrys bonded with her tonight, his aging would slow too, and they'd have a few hundred years of bonded bliss.

She broke the kiss, lifting the covers to invite him inside. Not only into her warm cocoon but also into her side and into her—eventually. The message from that faerie fecker and the business of goddesses could wait. Moments like these were far more important.

Emrys lined his body up next to hers, wrapping an arm about her naked waist and pulling her against him. He radiated more heat than she, so much he felt feverish at first, and he too was ready for her. He growled as their bodies fitted into one another, lock and key. "I adore that there's no bullshit about not seeing the bride on the wedding day. "

Myla pulled him back to her lips. Their bodies began to move as they shared more long and leisurely kisses. Emrys lifted a hand and cupped her breast, rolling a nipple between his thumb and forefinger, and Myla mewled into his mouth. She arched her back and had to break the kiss to catch her breath. "Em," she said with an exhale.

He trailed his way down her neck and replaced his fingers with his mouth, suckling her peaked nipple deeply. Myla pressed upward into him, thrashing her head on the pillow. Her body jerked with every stroke of his tongue. She let out a long "oohhh," bit her lip, and furrowed her brows as pure pleasure radiated straight to her core. When he released her, he started to move down her body, but she stopped him. "No. I'm ready now."

"But—"

Myla put a finger across his lips. She adored when he kissed her nether lips, but not now. She felt too much urgency, too much need to be full of this man. "I want you inside when I come."

With a wicked grin, Emrys rolled onto his back, pulling her on top of him. Myla felt his cock between her legs, engorged and ready. She kissed each of his nipples, relishing the small growls he emitted under her ministrations too. Reaching between her legs, she stroked the length of him, using his pre-cum to ease the strokes. She watched his face as his eyes closed and he lost himself in her touch. When she toyed with the spot near the head of his cock—the one that always made him squirm— Emrys let out an open-mouthed moan. Myla smirked, having him rising toward climax already. Exactly where she wanted him, but then again, she didn't want to push him over the edge just yet. She rubbed his cock between her folds, and then positioned him at her core and waited.

When he opened his eyes, looking almost pained with desire, she placed both hands on his abs and sank down ever-so-slowly. His size forced her to take him little-by-little so her body could adjust. But when he was fully sheathed inside her, she felt so very full. Stretched. They paused for a long moment before the need to move overwhelmed her. She leaned forward and gave Emrys a deep kiss, then started to rock. He held her close with strong arms until their pace naturally quickened. Myla pushed herself to sitting, riding him and gaining the leverage to slide farther up and return to him in long, excruciatingly delicious strokes. Emrys thrust his hips upward, moving opposite her then meeting her again in the middle. Their tempo sped away-together-away but always connected until both were making tiny ecstasy-filled sounds with every meeting. He pushed a hand between them, circling Myla's clit with his thumb, and tension gathered in Myla's lower belly.

"So close," she breathed.

"Yes," he answered.

And then, all her muscles locked up and she couldn't maintain control. Hot liquid flowed throughout her as her release slammed into her. Emrys's grip around her waist kept her from toppling as he pushed upward twice more then sat up, embraced her, and roared with his own orgasm. They remained sitting, embracing, buried in one another for a time Myla couldn't count, but their love and passion flowed through her and between them.

When the waves of pleasure had passed, she lolled her head onto his shoulder and wrapped her legs around him. She never wanted to release him from within her or from her embrace. Thoughts, or maybe dreams, about their bonding ceremony later that night warmed her mind and heart. Emrys stroked her bare back, but the silence between them felt more comfortable than any speech could break.

Eventually, a shadow of light crept back into her mind, and she looked around the dark room suddenly. "Did you hear that?"

Emrys kissed her beneath the earlobe. "What?"

She released a long breath, certain she'd heard the distinctive *tling, tling* that had accompanied Danu's words the evening before. "It must be my imagination reminding me of the message Malin and I have to deliver."

Her shoulders drooped. She didn't want to get up and shower yet, but it *was* a rare thing when a goddess sought someone out to deliver a message. She owed it to Aodh to deliver it quickly. Myla rolled out of Emrys's lap and toward the edge of the bed. Her pháirtí tossed the covers and jumped up before she could stand.

"Let me care for you," he said, striding toward the bathroom. Lithe and beautiful, Emrys wasn't a large man, but he was her idea of perfection. Seconds later, the shower started.

Emrys returned, offering her a hand. He often did this after their coupling—bathed her and fed her as if worshiping her. When she'd asked about it, he'd told her simply, "To show you I'm worthy of you," as if it were the most natural thing in the world for a human to say to a dark witch, one of the Dracagard. Myla could recall their first meeting at the hospital in the daylight realm. Some faceless human had insisted she see a doctor for a twisted ankle, and Emrys had been the one working the ER that night. They'd entered into what she had believed an affair, meeting almost nightly for months after his shift in the hours before dawn when she had to return to the Penumbra. He never questioned her leaving, and she'd let him believe it was for her to get to a day job. It'd been five and a half months before he'd spoken of worth. And when he'd said those words, Myla knew. Emrys was her pháirtí. It was the first time she'd imagined she would be bound in darkness.

And tonight . . . her dream would become reality.

MALIN

SISTER TO SISTER: TWO DARK HEARTS

I N PREPARATIONS FOR THE CEREMONY, Malin braided her sister's hair, loosening each loop so it would appear softer than the tightly plaited styles they normally wore when visiting the human domain to fight their foes— the semaphors. Tonight was about Myla's bonding and committing herself to her mate for the remainder of their days and into the life beyond. A serious but happy occasion that deserved her full intention.

Malin tried to focus on the joy her sister radiated, but her mind kept wandering back to the events of the night before. Danu's message and Raine's warning had her head spinning. But Aodh's distinct absence when they'd visited Dark Haven to deliver Danu's message had also troubled her. True, when they'd inscribed the message onto parchment and placed into the eternal blue flame burning in the sacred chalice, there'd been no question as to if it would reach the Dark Mother. However, they'd received no reply from Aodh. It confused Malin why the Fae Goddess would appear to them, but the Dark goddess didn't. And then, there was another, more personal question she'd been trying to ignore.

She peered up at her sister's image reflected in the glass, so familiar to her. Unlike Malin, Myla wore a smile that seemingly wouldn't dissipate.

"Can I ask you something?" Malin asked.

Myla's eyes went wide. "Of course. Anything."

Malin focused on her work rather than looking directly at her sister. "Emrys is wonderful."

"That's hardly a question."

"Fair." She tucked a braid and slipped another pin in to hold it in place. "But I need you to know I'm not questioning your choice in mate."

There had been men before in Malin's life, both human and wiccan. She had enjoyed their company, yet she'd never had cause to consider any might be her pháirtí. Thus, even though she witnessed her sister's pull toward the man she would bond with this night, Malin couldn't quite fathom how the connection truly felt.

The faerie's words replayed in her mind. *There will be someone strong in your future . . . a match for your soul and you'll be a balm for one another's rage.* Malin blinked several times. She had so many questions about Raine's warning. Or was it a promise? Regardless, in the light of Danu's missive to Aodh and Myla's bonding, she couldn't find it in herself to share the faerie's prediction with her twin. "What I'm wondering is . . . have you ever had doubts?"

"Oh, Mal." Myla shot her a soft, caring look in the mirror.

Malin rolled her eyes and reached for the hair spray.

Afterward, Myla stood and grasped both her hands. "I never thought about it when Emrys and I began our trysts in the beginning, but once I knew, I never doubted.

He has never given me cause." She paused, squeezing Malin's hands. "You'll find your mate soon; I can feel it. It will be before Mother leaves this world for Nèamh, and"—Myla's radiance dimmed—"we're starting to see the signs of her final aging. But we have time; she will see us both mated before that comes. And when you meet him, you will know too."

The mention of their mother, the high priestess of their coven, passing caused Malin to lower her brows and pinch her lips. Why did her sister have to remind her about the ancient predictions from the seers?

Myla tilted her head, narrowing her eyes. "You look angry."

"Not angry. Concerned, perhaps." She took a deep breath. "If the birth of wiccan twins is truly the omen they foretold—a big if, mind you—then Mother's passing will mean too much for me to think about. Maybe if I don't find my pháirtí, we won't have to worry about such things."

"Mal—"

"I know." She threw up a hand to halt her sister's chiding. "Natural things will happen regardless of my resistance. None of that matters tonight. Let's get you dressed." Malin pulled Myla toward the adjacent room where their attire for the ceremony waited.

Myla's deep red gown glimmered with violet hues as it reflected the characteristic dark blue of the Penumbra. Her matching sheer cloak, beneath which her dragon Aemro would coil about her waist, hung next to the gown. Lastly, an overcloak imbued with darkness by the Aodh's Darklings would be the final layer to the bridal ensemble. On a separate rack, Malin's unadorned dress and a cloak with embroidered Serch Bythol symbols around the hem awaited her, Myla's witness for the ceremony.

When both were dressed, Malin scanned her sister from head to toe. Her eyes prickled at the sight, and she opened her mouth to speak.

But Myla lifted the skirts and rushed over, arms open. "I want to"—she swallowed as if she too felt the burn of immanent tears—"say I love you and thank you for honoring me by witnessing my union tonight."

Damn the elaborate gown and cloaks; Malin crushed her sister into an embrace. "I wouldn't let anyone else stand for you. We are two dark hearts born of one mother, and this is how it should be. Always."

Myla squeezed her in return.

Malin sniffed and pulled back a little. "Okay." They smiled and chuckled together. "We can't cry now," Malin said as the door opened.

Both looked; Myla's Aemro and Malin's dragon, Breyze, glided into the room together. Myla opened her cloaks, and Aemro encircled her waist a deep green belt dividing the red of her gown. Before settling, he lifted his snout and bit into her wrist. The dark magic flowing into her veins had Myla closing her eyes and inhaling slowly, deeply. Seconds later, Breyze did the same with Malin, and the relief of the magic infusion from her dragon made her quiver.

Their mother, Minerva, entered after the dragons. She wore a black cloak, hood raised with her hair flowing over one shoulder. The depth of the black and the dark magic woven into its fibers accented the ever-increasing number of white strands within her thick black hair. She spread her arms, begging them to come to her.

Minerva's voice intoned centuries of wisdom, as if

beginning to crack with age at the edges, as she said, "My daughters."

"It is time," Malin said. "Ready?"

Myla nodded, and they walked together toward Minerva.

Their mother softly stroked Myla's cheek. "So much beauty." Then she lifted Malin's chin. "And power." She hugged them to her, one in each arm. "You both make a mother proud."

EMRYS

BEST MAN

TWILIGHT HAD TURNED TO FULL darkness, but Wickney's restaurants and stores were still turning a good business by the time Emrys made it to Sacred Heart Catholic Church to meet his best man, Godric. He stared up at the cathedral's ornate façade for several minutes before marching up the steps and into the sanctuary. His oldest friend in the world, Godric Laferty, knelt at the altar, face lifted to the spot-lit cross with a crucified Christ on display. As Emrys padded down the aisle between the red velvet-cushioned pews, his friend folded his hands and bowed his head, clearly not seeing Emrys enter or approach him.

Godric prayed quietly but aloud. "Watch over my friend Emrys Murray this night, for I fear he enters a world untouched by your grace, dear Lord."

Emrys cleared his throat, and Godric clamored to stand. "How long have you—"

"I just arrived." They embraced in a half-hug, then Emrys added, "I appreciate your prayers, but I believe with all my heart that Myla is good, just another of your

Lord's creatures who he watches over, as do all the gods."

Godric looked at the floor. "There is only one God, Emrys."

"Very well," he answered, not wanting to have this argument again. For the most part, they'd come to terms with their differing beliefs. They'd both been raised Catholic, but after his parents' death, Emrys lost what little faith he'd had. Godric, on the other hand . . . Well, Emrys supposed that this night, when he would promise himself to his love, struck a chord with his faithful friend. As one of the institutions the Catholic Church held sacred, he may defile the sacrament of marriage by the commitment he was about to make. At least in the eyes of the devout.

"I hope for your sake that you're right in your assessment. Still, I will pray for you." Godric said.

Emrys pursed his lips, glancing up at the cross accented with gold. He looked around at the statues, also dressed in gold-trimmed clothing and adorned with jewels. And the stained glass, thousands of colors soldered painstakingly together. Too much wealth was tied up in this institution for his taste. "Let's grab a coffee before it's time, okay?"

"Sure."

Together they walked to the exit where Godric stopped. He dipped his fingers into the water behind the last pew and crossed himself before leaving. As they descended the steps, Emrys said, "Despite our differences, I appreciate you witnessing for me tonight."

Godric made a small sound but said little more.

At the coffee shop two blocks down, they both ordered and sat at a table near the window. The alley where they'd meet the Darkling in an hour was just around the corner, so they had a little time to chat.

"How's your father?" Emrys asked, removing the lid from his Americano.

"Doing as well as can be expected. Some days he's himself, and it seems the Alzheimer's never touched him. Others, well . . . he calls me by his oldest brother's name. And he's having more and more challenges with blood clots."

"Must be difficult. Do you need any help?"

Godric blew on his drink and took a sip. "Nah. The facility he's in has the best medical and mental health care in a hundred miles of Wickney. Outside of that, I'm working with a lawyer on the power of attorney so I can sell the farm. That should pay for the remainder of his care and more. Soon enough, he'll be in God's hands."

Emrys reached over and touched his friend's arm, a bedside manner–habit he'd developed over the years. "You know I'm here. All you have to do is call or text, and I'll be there as soon as I can."

His friend pulled away, a moment of pain crossing his eyes, then waved his hand. "Now's not the time to harp on it. It must blow to not have either of your parents around for your wedding."

"Bonding." Emrys corrected his friend. His mom and dad had died in a car crash his first year of college, so they'd missed almost all the big moments in his life: graduating, finishing med school, landing his position at the Wickney University Medical Center ER. "But I'm accustomed to it. You're my connection to our childhood on the farms now." He raised his coffee.

They toasted.

While Emrys had lost touch with almost everyone

from his childhood, Godric had kept his connections to the people they'd attended school within the rural school system twenty miles west of Wickney. They filled the time chatting about happenings "back home" until the clock in Emrys's periphery showed they only had about ten minutes remaining.

Standing, Emrys said, "I hope I've prepared you. This ceremony will be strange. However, there will be no reception to keep you up late, so you can be bright-eyed for all your IT business tomorrow." Emrys threw a few dollars on the table for the cleanup, and they left.

A rat scurried by and Godric started, hand flying to cover his chest. Then he settled, but still seemed on edge as they turned into the alley and went deeper until the dark almost obscured all the city lights. "Are you sure about this, Emrys?" And then it went black, as if all streetlights and moonlight were controlled by the flip of a switch.

Godric gasped.

Emrys took his arm with one hand and hushed his friend. He pulled out a small vial and took a sip. The rotten orange taste made the corners of his mouth pinch, but it passed. After a few more seconds, his eyes began to see shapes within the darkness highlighted by hues of blue. "Here. Take a sip. Tastes like shit, but it'll help you see."

Godric's eyes were stretched wide—the kind of reaction most people have when they enter a dark theater. He gave a nod and blindly reached out a hand.

Emrys placed the vial in is palm.

His friend tipped it back and gagged after swallowing. He doubled over, coughed, and sputtered but didn't throw it up.

Emrys patted him on the back until he could stand again. "Just a tonic to help your eyes adjust."

After a few more minutes, Godric scanned the alley with awe spreading on his face just as . . .

A hooded figure stepped through the wall and marched toward them.

MALIN

BOUND IN DARKNESS

AT MYLA'S SIDE, MALIN WAITED in still silence for the ceremony to begin. They'd gathered near the Awen—the ancient symbol representing harmony between opposites of the universe. It marked barriers between the Dark realm and other adjacent realms. At present, the three concentric circles glowed blue around a hazy window into the human realm, or Earth. Beyond the Awen, three figures gathered. The one with his back to the Awen was Branok, marked by his acolyte robes as a Darkling of Aodh. The Darklings were fewer in modern times as the number of wiccan rituals had diminished over time. But tonight, Branok had assumed the sacred duty to aid Emrys through the binding ceremony.

Myla's pháirtí and a slightly taller, broader-shouldered man, surely Emrys's witness, faced the Darkling. The man was no one Malin had ever met, and although his figure was somewhat wavy while looking through the portal, he seemed attractive—sharp features, a keen gaze, and the close-cropped hair she favored over Emrys's shoulder-length cut. She shifted her weight, uncomfortable at the strange observation.

Sound didn't penetrate the barrier, but the three had their heads bowed together in deep conversation. Branok likely issued instructions and answered what questions were permissible for the men regarding what would happen during the ritual. On the Dark side of the portal, Malin and her mother stood with Myla, waiting a few paces behind Darkling Jareth, the second presiding acolyte and the one who would support Myla. Once they received the cue, they'd walk through the portal into the human realm. The Awen would remain activated and open until the close of the first rites, at which time when all present returned to the Penumbra.

Malin waited, feeling heavy in her gut. Small aches twinged in her joints and muscles, the kind that begged her to launch into motion. She couldn't figure out why she felt so on edge. She supported tonight's union with all her heart, wanted nothing more for Myla than the happiness and anticipation she could sense rolling off her twin. If it wasn't for Malin's role in this ceremony, she'd return to the coven's manor and scry, or read her Tarot, in an attempt to learn the cause of her unease. But those efforts would have to wait, for she had a service to perform for her sister and, ultimately, a duty to her coven.

When Darkling Branok took his place at Emrys's side and all three faced the opening between realms, Jareth motioned Minerva forward. Malin's mother stepped forward, holding a small carafe and two goblets. Together, she and Jareth walked through the portal. Malin gave her sister one last hug and followed. Everyone save for Myla formed a semicircle around the Awen—Minerva, then the Darklings, then Emrys, the new person, and finally, Malin.

The alley in Wickney where the portal opened was normally a rundown crack between buildings with a distinct stench of urine. Although tonight, Branok had performed his first task beautifully. The spell he'd cast made it seem like they stood in a cozy room with brocade-covered walls and plush carpet. The serenity of the alley's new appearance did nothing to quell Malin's itch to fly into action. If anything, standing next to the stranger and smelling his addictive scent of fresh tobacco, cinnamon, and wood made her flight response so much worse.

Emrys leaned forward, peering around the man toward Malin. "This is Godric Laferty, my oldest friend."

She exchanged a smile and nod with Godric a second before the Awen shimmered and released Myla into the human realm. Her sister glided forward, cloaks swaying about her as she moved. Malin turned her head to watch Emrys, whose eyes widened and mouth spread into a grin as he took in the sight of his mate. Myla's smile mirrored her pháirtí's, unfading.

Minerva turned to face the others with her back toward the Awen, and the Darklings arranged the rest of the attendants. Myla and Emrys faced Minerva, a Darkling to their outer sides, and Malin stood beside Godric in the couple's proverbial shadows. The small twinges in her muscles began to burn hotter, like lightning coursing through her body. Even as she began to wonder if Godric was causing this reaction, Malin fought to ignore the urge to turn and give him her full attention.

Focus on Myla, she scolded herself.

Using his official-sounding voice, Branok said, "Emrys Murry, is it your will to bind your spirit to this woman, a wiccan of Darkness?"

Emrys replied, "It is my will."

Jareth asked the similar question of Myla, and she replied in kind.

Minerva lifted the carafe. "I ask the Dark Mother's blessing on the willowwood wine that it may act as a balm for this couple and ease their pains of bonding." She poured the amber liquid.

Godric glanced sideways at Malin at the mention of pains, and she stiffened. Emrys wouldn't know the details of the ritual, but surely, he would have explained that it was no blissful wedding. Wouldn't he have?

Myla and Emrys encircled their arms and drank from the stoneware goblets. When done, the Darklings took the goblets from their hands.

"Take her hands," Branok instructed.

"Offer yours," Jareth said to Myla and waited for the couple to comply. "Now, you will enter the Penumbra together. This symbolizes accepting the bonds your mate will offer this night and wear them proudly for your natural lives and as you pass into Nèamh."

Minerva stepped to the side, allowing the couple to pass first, then she followed. The Darklings ushered Malin and Godric through next. Within the Darkness, Godric gasped and grabbed Malin's hand. Electricity shot up her arm; she inhaled sharply and recoiled from his touch. What had that been? And why did she want to try it again? She rubbed her palm as Branok and Jareth came into the Penumbra after them. Small sounds of whispered spells told her that one of the two closed the portal behind them.

Malin whispered to Godric, "Don't be afraid. Your part in the ceremony won't last long, and I'll see you back to the other side."

Godric rubbed the center of his chest, visibly trying to settle himself. The man's eyes darted this way and that, taking in the setting that was a mirror to Wickney itself, only dark and highlighted in blue hues. Malin recalled the first time she'd entered and what a wonder it had been. Then, though, there had been no cities. She'd entered through the largest stone at the Beltany circle in northern Ireland. Still, it had racked her senses, and she gave Godric credit for not crumpling under the onslaught of new sensations. The combination of this ceremony and an introduction to the realm of Darkness were so different from his own.

Mother gathered Myla and Emrys before her.

The Darklings turned Emrys and Myla to face one another and urged them onto their knees.

"Bow your heads," Minerva said, then placed a hand on the backs of their necks. "Under the gaze of the Dark Mother, *grá síoraí*," she bellowed, the spell for sealing a bond between two people ringing in Malin's ears.

Under her touch, both tensed and hissed on a shared sharp inhale.

Dark magic glowed blue between Minerva's fingers. "Long and slow breaths, children. Allow those breaths and the wine to soothe the pain." She closed her eyes, lifting her face as she allowed the magic to flow through her and brand the couple with the most ancient of their symbols, the Serch Bythol.

Love eternal.

The process only lasted a matter of minutes, but the entire time, Malin felt Godric's gaze upon her—worried and questioning. She held his hand in an attempt to keep him calm, but eventually had to do something to tame his fear. Under her breath, she said, "Breyze," begging her dragon for the venom that'd allow her to access the Darkness. Fangs pierced her at the wrist, and she whispered, "*Socair*" to calm Godric. The loosening of his grip on her fingers let her know it'd worked, but she allowed a small trickle of magic to maintain the spell on him. If he was panicking over this little, the next part would rock him to his core.

By the time the magic had done its work on Myla and Emrys, they were both breathing heavily, but love radiated between them as they stared into one another's eyes. Branok and Jareth helped them to stand.

Jareth removed Myla's cloak, revealing Aemro. "Myla, daughter of Minerva, you may release your Draca."

Although they'd surely met before, Branok introduced the dragon to Emrys, "This is Aemro, Myla's bonded familiar." The small, snake-like dragon slithered from around Myla's waist and hovered in the air between them. "Do you accept him as a part of this union, knowing Myla is oath bound to serve the Draca as a member of the Dracagard?"

"I do."

"Present Aemro with your wrist," Branok instructed to Emrys.

When Emrys did, Aemro struck. Emrys stumbled, arched his spine backward. Branok, well-prepared for the reaction, caught him and held him upright as the venom coursed through Emrys's veins toward his heart. It would be poison to him, save for the marque signifying everlasting love Minerva had just placed on the back of his neck. As it was, he simply needed to adapt. And having been bitten, he would never again have need of the dark-vision tonic while in the Penumbra, but like all other wiccans, he'd be overly sensitive to daylight if in the human realm. And journeying to Faerie would never be in his future.

As Emrys's body jerked several more times, Godric's

hand gripped tighter onto Malin.

Her fingers tingled and started to go numb, so she intensified the flow of magic. "I'll explain all this when they've gone. Soon," she said quietly. Even as the words left her lips, her mind reeled. Explaining meant she would go with him into the human realm—something she wouldn't normally desire. She felt his pull. How? She couldn't understand.

"The second rite is complete, the binding sealed," said Branok, "Myla, Aemro will take you both and introduce Emrys to the nest to complete the third and final rite."

"Yet, before they leave us," Jareth added, "we address our witnesses. Malin, daughter of Minerva, do you stand for Myla and bear witness to her love for this man?"

"I do," Malin answered.

Branok then asked, "Godric Laferty, do you stand for Emrys Murray in this union?"

Malin released his hand, suddenly breaking the magical flow. The spell still lived, but unless they touched skin-to-skin, he would feel nothing of her power. She didn't want to influence his answer. Emrys looked pleadingly at his friend, as if begging him to offer his approval.

Godric hesitated, his brows peaked. The wandering hand drifted back up to his chest, and he cast his eyes downward. How many thoughts must have been running through his mind? But eventually, he sighed. "I do."

Grinning with his elation, Emrys swept Myla into his arms and spun her around. When he set her back onto her feet, they bowed and curtsied with poise and walked away hand-in-hand.

Jareth thanked Minerva, and Branok declared, "The Draca owns the last rite. This concludes your part in the

Dark Bonding." The Darklings tucked their hands into their sleeves like monks, bowed their heads, and began walking in the direction of Dark Haven.

Malin went to her mother. "I'll return Godric."

Minerva leaned in, green eyes flashing with warning. "Clean him, darling." She looked at the man over Malin's shoulder. "Something's . . . off with him."

Malin pressed her lips together and nodded noncommittally. "I'll see you soon." She spun on her heel, facing Godric. Panic seemed to rise on his face again as her calming spell had been absent for too long. She offered her hand. "Ready?"

Godric looked at her. Then at her hand. He appeared relieved when he accepted her offer.

She guided him back to the Awen, and Malin traced the three concentric circles until they glowed with Dark magic and the window opened again. She tilted her head and stepped inside, pulling him through the portal.

RAINE

MOTHER CALLS

THE WEEKEND FOLLOWING HIS ENCOUNTER with the thruple and Aodh's witches, Raine returned to his autumn gig at the Ren Fest with hopes of a profitable—and uneventful—weekend. At one point during the week, the puzzle around the body he'd seen in his memory walk niggled at him enough that he'd visited the police department to find his favorite detective, Kennedi Craine. Unfortunately, she had been off for the week, taking her mother to Chicago or Vegas . . . or was it Phuket?

Eh. He shrugged. Unimportant details.

Although, luck had been on his side when he received the greater honor of a "workout" with one of Ken's junior officers, Harley Gold, at the WPD gym. As with all the other times, Raine had "worked out" with them, he'd glamoured and nudged his way through the hour, lifting the minimal weight while using his Fae nature to trick Harley into believing he thrived on the rush following taxing his muscles to the fullest. *Ha!* What he actually lived for in those moments was siphoning off a little of Harley's levity over their own physical prowess.

Damn, he missed hanging with Harley on the regular! However, with what he'd seen in his memory walk last weekend, he'd be tight with them again soon. And Ken and Vic too. This puzz—er case was going to be the best fun he'd had since, well, the La Pointe murder case.

Raine trudged up the hill toward the festival grounds, carrying a new banner for his show under one arm. With every step, he smirked a little more with anticipation. It was still several minutes until the opening cannon blast when he arrived on the lawn outside the gates. A costumed crowd waited for the king and queen of the realm to stand on the wall and announce the time. He wove his way through the after-the-nine-to-five crowd, inhaling their giddiness as he went. He entered the festival grounds through the exit to the far side. Other performers and shopkeepers milled around inside already. Raine exchanged *"good morrows"* and *"how fare ye-s"* as he passed on his way to his cart.

Energy thrummed in the air and raised the hairs on his arms. Friday nights were his favorite days to assume his *Raine of Fortune* persona—only three hours, but when humans wanted to decompress, they were at their most receptive to his wiles. Every Friday night devolved into a huge party, and being the only kid-free day, things sometimes got a little racy.

Reaching the wagon, he unrolled his banner, draped it from the pole on the side of the cart, and stood back to take in the whole of his stage. He pursed his lips and said to the image of himself, glamoured of course, "Lookin' great!"

The cannon blasted; cheers and a din of voices muddled the air. Raine threw open his doors for business, but before he could turn and begin hawking the crowd . . .

"Hello, Brother." The accursed Fae prince, Trevon

of Queen Amaryllis, Raine's brother, and the one still in their mother's good graces verily glowed within the cart.

Raine glanced around then clamored inside, shutting the door behind him. He crossed his arms and glared at the faerie. "What in the name of Danu are you doing here?"

Trevon toyed with a wand, one of Raine's many props. "Do humans really believe in this shite?"

Circling to the back side of his small table, Raine grumbled. "You've never spent much time in this realm, have you?"

"Why ever would I put myself through that much pain?" Trevon dropped the wand on the table as if it were a dead and rotting animal. He wiped his unglamoured, three-fingered hands onto the velvet cloth covering Raine's crystal ball. "Mother knows you spoke to Aodh's wiccans."

Raine glared at his brother. Of course he'd be bringing news from Amaryllis. That seemed to be his only interest in these modern times. Raine despised that Trevon and his formerly betrothed faerie, Briar thirsted so much for power. And then he recalled the message Danu had conveyed to the crabby witch: *There will be a shift between Light and Dark.* Did that mean . . .? Raine waved his hand in the air flippantly. "And what interest does the Queen of the Fae have in that?"

Trevon lifted his chin to peer down his long nose at Raine. "Mother cannot see the nature of the conversation."

Reclining in his chair, Raine propped his feet on the desk and steepled his fingers in front of his chin. He mused, *Ifrinn, it would be nice to have a single-malt Scotch in hand at the moment.* At least the burn from that would wash away the nasty taste his brother was leaving in his mouth. "Still. I fail to find purpose in your visit."

"Is her concern truly not obvious?"

"Can't say that it is. Mother and I clearly do not see things in the same light. Is that not obvious after the last time I was in Faerie? Oh! Yes, that's right, she banished me to Aodh's Dark Domain." Raine blinked slowly, sighing. "Just tell me why you're here, Trevon. And leave."

"Queen Amaryllis wants to know what you're planning with the witches."

Raine furrowed his brow. Did they truly not see Danu's hand in the matter? "I have no plan."

"It is very un-Fae of you to not have a plan." His brother quirked a brow.

Keep your mouth sealed, Raine thought. It wasn't the first time Trevon had accused him of such, and Raine was beginning to believe it wasn't his Fae nature his brother was questioning. Maybe it was that he didn't bend to his mother's narrow expectations. Perhaps, the shift Danu had mentioned involved his dear mother and her position as Queen of Faerie. He narrowed his eyes at Trevon. Could that be true?

Receiving no reply, Trevon continued, "Mother is also infuriated that you and your detective have stolen a noble from her court. She bids you to come to court to answer for your, shall we say, continued transgression."

"I have *stolen* no one from Mother."

"Is that true, brother-dearest?" Trevon's voice sounded smooth, calm, but it held a note of scorn.

Maybe it wasn't entirely true. He'd gone back into Faerie after Kennedi's *becoming* and promptly returned her to the human realm. But Kennedi was only half Fae, so why would his mother consider that a theft from her court? Raine ground his teeth then said, "Maybe not entirely, but Mother has seen to it that I am no longer welcome in Fae, that I cannot see our sister in Sanctuary, and that I have no choice in who I take as a mate. I'm tired of her schemes. So you can return to Amaryllis and the two of you can work your petty machinations, but do leave me out of this . . . *Brother.*"

Voices sounded outside the cart.

Raine perked. "Glamour up," he said as the door to his cart flew open. Trevon was quick about disguising himself from the humans.

A good thing because a mortal man in a jester's costume rushed inside—a festival performer, but not one Raine knew. "Raine?"

He sat forward, a grin spreading across his face and hands held wide. "The one and only."

Trevon snickered, and Raine shot him another sour look.

Jester panted—winded from rushing over?—huffed, then said, "You have connections at WPD, right?"

Turning to look at the performer sideways, he drawled, "I do."

"There's a"—Jester glanced at Trevon—"an um matter, um, behind the Witchery Shoppe."

Raine stood abruptly. "Well, I'm done here." He ushered the man outside, ignoring his brother. When they were at a safe enough distance, he whispered. "What kind of matter?"

"A, um, body." His eyes shifted around the crowd as if to make certain no one heard.

"Shite! Let's go." On the way, Raine pulled out his

phone, pressing the side button. He waited for the bell sound and used the voice command: "Text Ken."

The robotic high-pitched voice answered,W "Do you mean. Kenn-edi Craine?"

"Yes!"

The bell on the phone sounded again as they rounded the back of the building to the Witchery Shoppe.

"Shite!" Raine yelled again, his stomach twisting at the sight of all the blood. A stench reached his nostrils, and he felt woozy and sweaty. "That's . . . Margo." He gagged, held onto the building, anWd barfed.

In the background his phone's voice replied, "I'm sorry. I don't recognize your message. Would you like to try again?"

* * *

READ MORE ABOUT RAINE'S ADVENTURES and bumbling murder investigations in *Raine of Fire*: https://books2read. com/Raine-of-Fire

READ MORE ABOUT MALIN AND Myla in *Fight For Darkness*, part of the Realm of Darkness boxset, October 4, 2022. https://books2read.com/RealmOfDarknessset

* * *

VISIT SUSAN'S WEBSITE: HTTPS://SUSANSTRADIOTTO. COM

SIGN UP FOR SUSAN'S NEWSLETTER: https://www. subscribepage.com/susansfantasycommunity